The Milkshake Man

Written by Sally Cole
Illustrated by Lorenzo Van Der Lingen

It was a very hot day. Dad, Millie, and I had been playing in the park.

"I'm worn out," said Dad. "Let's have a rest over there, and then we'll get milkshakes from the Milkshake Man."

We lay on the grass by the Milkshake Man's van. It was painted like a rainbow. I wished we could have a cool milkshake right now...

...but a spaceship glided down.

3

A door opened and a little man stepped out. His hair, his beard, his suit, and his shoes were all white. The little man looked like a milkshake.

"I come from the planet Milkshake," he said. "Would you and Millie like to come and play? These milkshakes will make you so small that you'll fit in my spaceship."

We said yes and drank the milkshakes.

We got smaller and smaller, until we were small enough to climb up the steps of the spaceship. Millie and I sat in big, soft marshmallow seats with licorice seat belts. Zoom! The spaceship whizzed off.

In no time at all, the spaceship landed with a big bump and we all got out.

"Come on," said the Milkshake Man. "I want to show you the milkshake cows."

We got into a chocolate space buggy and went along a road until we saw a green, mint field. The field was full of sugar daisies and rainbow cows. Next to each cow was a matching pail. Millie and I were amazed, we'd never seen anything like this before.

"Come on," said the Milkshake Man. "Sit down and milk a cow. A fresh milkshake will come out. Drink as much as you like, then we'll go to Ice Cream Mountain."

Ice Cream Mountain was enormous! It was so high, the top of it was hidden in a candy-pink cloud. The Milkshake Man gave us some toffee skis and a chocolate snowboard. We got on a chairlift and went up the mountain.

"Eat all you want," said the Milkshake Man, when we got to the top. "Ice Cream Mountain never melts and everything just keeps growing."

Millie and I reached up and nibbled the clouds. We ate our snowboards and we ate ice cream off Ice Cream Mountain. Millie and I had so much fun, but we didn't have time to ski.

All too soon, the Milkshake Man said, "It's time to go back to your dad."

The Milkshake Man, Millie, and I went back to the spaceship. We sat back in our big, soft marshmallow seats with licorice seat belts and zoomed off.

As the spaceship landed, the Milkshake Man gave us both a purple milkshake.

"Drink this," he said, "and you'll be big again."

As Millie and I drank the purple milkshakes, we slowly grew back to our full sizes again.

"Thank you. We've had a great time," Millie and I called to the Milkshake Man.

"I'll see you again at my rainbow van," said the Milkshake Man and he waved good–bye.

"Why are you saying 'thank you'?" said Dad. "We haven't had our milkshakes yet. Let's go and get them now."

Dad was surprised when Millie and I said we didn't want a milkshake.

"Well I want one," he said. "I'm going to have a milkshake and an ice cream. Are you sure that you don't want one?"

But the Milkshake Man was not surprised when Millie and I didn't have anything.

He smiled and said, "Come back another day. You may feel like a milkshake or an ice cream when you haven't been visiting other planets!"

Millie and I just smiled and looked at each other!